No More Peanuts For Ellie the Elephant

A Children's Coloring Book on Peanut Allergies

CHRISTINE E. CIRILLO

DEDICATION:

To Patrick and Lilian Kerner,

our two newest members of the family.

Ellie the Elephant lived at the zoo,

Right next to her friend Kenny, the Kangaroo.

At lunch time Ellie and Kenny always ate alone,

At the "Peanut-Free Zone".

One day a little girl named Suzie came along.

She wanted to feed the elephants peanuts,

... *which was very, very wrong.*

Suzie gave peanuts to all the elephants at the zoo,

Even Ellie, had a peanut too...

A few minutes later,

Ellie got a very itchy rash...

which became greater and greater.

And as Ellie's reaction spread,

Her trunk and tongue became all swollen and red.

Ellie rushed to her mommy,

With a strange pain in her tummy.

Ellie's trunk started to close,

And then...

Her vet came rushing over with a magic pen.

The vet used all of his force, oh my!

And swung the pen into Ellie's outer thigh.

He slowly counted

1... 2... 3...

And dropped it far away from Ellie.

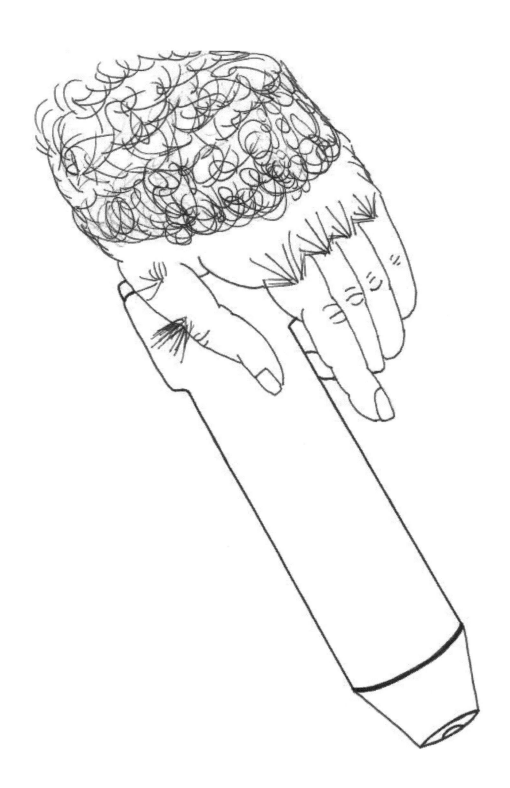

Ellie started feeling much, much better...

And now she knows why she can never eat a peanut again,

...or even Peanut Butter!

INFORMATION FOR PARENTS:

A peanut allergy is very serious; Symptoms can range from mild to severe. Be alert to warning signs. For example: A child may say, *"my tongue (or lips) feel tingly"* after eating a certain food. This is a reason to seek medical follow-up.

Know your child's symptoms. Teach your child about his or her allergy. They are never too young to learn. Read all food labels and teach your child this habit.

Inform all your child's care-givers, teachers, school nurse, friends, and their parents, of your child's allergy. This notification is very important, consider purchasing an allergy alert ID bracelet with your child's allergy listed.

Consult your child's pediatrician/physician on what medicine to administer with an allergic reaction. If an EpiPen® ("Magic Pen") is prescribed, learn how to use it, as well as all care-givers.

THE USE OF AN EPIPEN® IS FOR LIFE-THREATENING ANAPHYLAXIS[1].

YOU MUST CALL 911 IF YOUR CHILD IS HAVING AN ALLERGIC REACTION REQUIRING THE USE OF AN EPIPEN®.

PLEASE NOTE: EXPIRATION DATES ON THE EPIPEN® AND REPLACE AS NEEDED. MAKE SURE ALL KEY PERSONNEL INVOLVED WITH YOUR CHILD HAVE AN EPIPEN. ®

---

[1] Anaphylaxis: A severe, potentially life-threatening allergic reaction.

ACKNOWLEDGMENTS:

I want to thank all those who helped contribute to the making and publishing of this book.

Thanks to my well-respected Molloy College Nursing Professor, **Andrea Spatarella**, *DNP, RN, FNP-BC* for the inspiration in writing this children's book.

I am deeply indebted to my parents: **Elizabeth J. Cirillo**, *BSN, RN, CCRN*, and **Felix Cirillo**, *RN*. This book would not have been complete without all of your support, valuable ideas, annotations, and encouragement.

Special thanks to **Pedro Vilaca**, for the underlying encouragement in publishing this book.

To **Robert Cirillo**, and **Bart "*Uncle*"**, **Barbara, Bart Jr., Patrick and Helen, Ryan**, and **Ann Kerner**, thank you all so much for your love and support.

And last but not least, I am grateful for **CreateSpace**, my publisher, for enabling me to self-publish my very first book!

Made in the USA
Middletown, DE
04 February 2018